AVA in CODE LAND

Jess Hitchman and Gavin Cullen   Illustrated by Leire Martin

PLAY

FEIWEL AND FRIENDS
New York • mackids.com

For all the little coders who want to
change the world—you got this!

A Feiwel and Friends Book

An imprint of Macmillan Publishing Group, LLC

120 Broadway, New York, NY 10271

AVA IN CODE LAND. Text copyright © 2020 by Jess Hitchman and Gavin Cullen.
Illustrations copyright © 2020 by Leire Martin. All rights reserved. Printed in China by
RR Donnelley Asia Printing Solutions Ltd., Dongguan City, Guangdong Province.

Our books may be purchased in bulk for promotional, educational, or business use. Please
contact your local bookseller or the Macmillan Corporate and Premium Sales Department at
(800) 221-7945 ext. 5442 or by email at MacmillanSpecialMarkets@macmillan.com.

Library of Congress Cataloging-in-Publication Data

Names: Hitchman, Jess, author. | Cullen, Gavin, 1972–author. | Martin, Leire, illustrator.

Title: Ava in code land / written by Jess Hitchman and Gavin Cullen ; illustrated by Leire Martin.

Description: First edition. | New York : Feiwel and Friends, 2020.

Summary: When Max Hacksalot traps video game character Ava in the
"Game over" screen, she uses her coding skills to create a new level.

Identifiers: LCCN 2019018598 | ISBN 9781250316615 (hardcover)

Subjects: | CYAC: Computer programming—Fiction. |
Video games—Fiction. | Hacking—Fiction.

Classification: LCC PZ7.1.H583 Av 2020 | DDC [E]—dc23

LC record available at https://lccn.loc.gov/2019018598

Book design by Liz Dresner

Feiwel and Friends logo designed by Filomena Tuosto

First edition, 2020

1 3 5 7 9 10 8 6 4 2

mackids.com

Ava thought living in a computer game was pretty great.

If she didn't like something . . .

. . . she could just change it.

```
Moon.size = "large";
```

```
Sky.color = "purple";
```

```
Cupcakes.count = 1762;
```

But her favorite part was spending time with her best friend, Pixels. Even if he did have a habit of turning into the things he was scared of.

Like . . .

jellyfish,

Help!

broccoli,

Eeeek!

and stripy underpants.

Noooooooo!

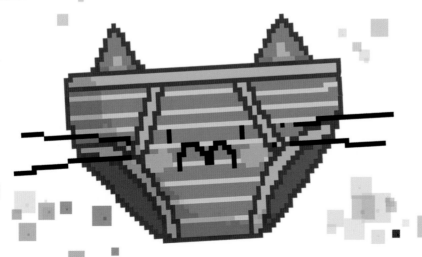

042073016

Ava spent every day coding her
world exactly the way she wanted it.

Level 1—Breakfast Roller Coaster

♥ × 600

Level 3—Birthday Every Day

Level 2—Underwater Disco

But not everything was perfect . . .

Max Hacksalot was the game's baddie. And he was a big . . . piratey . . . cheat . . .

HA HA ha ha arrrhhh!

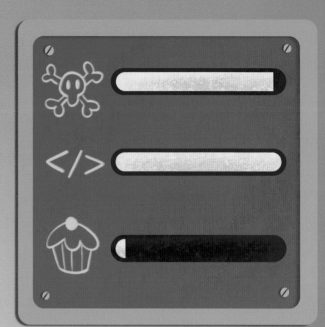

When Max got bored, he rode around the game (on his magical pirate unicorn) BREAKING bits of Ava's code.

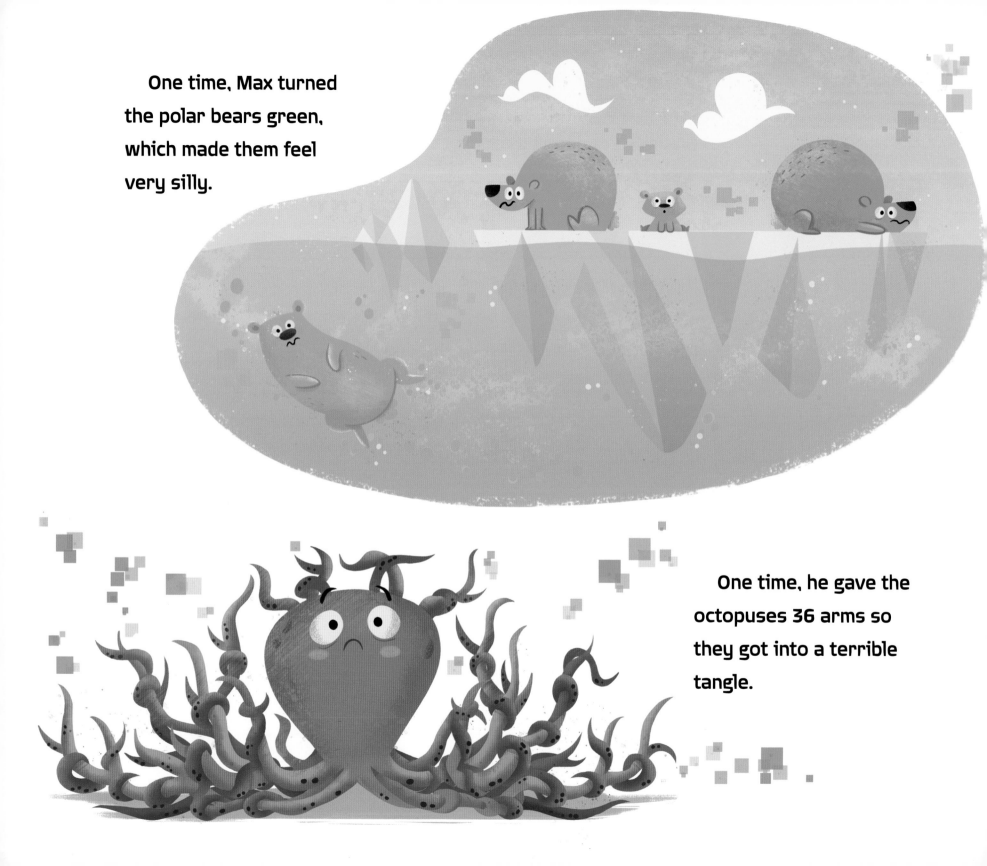

One time, Max turned the polar bears green, which made them feel very silly.

One time, he gave the octopuses 36 arms so they got into a terrible tangle.

And one time, he swapped the sound files so the dogs said "Tweet!" and the birds said "Woof!"

So every time, Ava had to find
the broken piece of code and fix it.

```
PolarBear.color = "white";
Octopus.arms = 8;
Bird.sound = "bird.m4a";
```

But one day, Max Hacksalot
went too far . . .

Ava woke up to find everything
around her was black.

GAME OVER

Max had *really* messed up her code this time,
and now she was trapped in the Game Over screen
with nothing but a really cute sad panda!

Ava slumped down against the giant *G*. All her hard work was lost, and there was *no way* she was starting again from the beginning.

But then she heard squares chattering. And she couldn't see Pixels anywhere.

So Ava began doing what she did best. Coding.

She started with some lights so she could find Pixels.

```
light_1 = {
        size: "small",
        color: "purple",
        effect: "glow",
        position: "top, left"
    };
```

```
light_2 = {
        size: "medium",
        color: "blue",
        brightness: 100,
        position: "center"
    };
```

Pixels lit up again. "Whoa, Ava! They look like planets!"

Ava's tummy rumbled. "And kind of like cakes too . . ."

And that gave her an excellent idea.

Ava wasn't going to let Max
decide how her game ended.
She deleted the Game Over
message and got to work building
a shiny new level in its place.

CaKe GalaXy

```
Title = "Game Over";
Title = "CAKE GALAXY";
```

Ava and Pixels coded (and giggled) all through the night until they had built the most delicious-y science-y Cake Galaxy level ever.

Pixels even got so used to being in the dark that he stopped being so scared of everything.

And he started turning into the things he was excited about instead.

Like . . .

spaceships,

Yay!

rainbows,

Wow!

and spotted socks.

Woo-hoo!

The finished Cake Galaxy level
was so much fun that EVERYONE
wanted to play.

Even . . .

000019510

Max Hacksalot's magical pirate unicorn!

Learning to code is great because it means you can make your ideas happen and build
things exactly how you want them—just like Ava. The code Ava uses in this story is based on
JavaScript. This programming language is used to make all kinds of games, apps, and websites.

A great way to get started with coding is with toys!

Here are a few of our favorites:

www.primotoys.com

www.terrapinlogo.com/products/robots.html

www.kano.me

www.techwillsaveus.com/shop

Then when you're ready to dive in deeper,

check out these websites:

www.codeclubworld.org/projects

www.gethopscotch.com

www.tynker.com

When you're learning to code, breaking stuff is just as important as making stuff.

So have fun and remember—it's only Game Over if you don't start playing.